BROKEN GIRLS

Broken Girls

A NOVEL

Tess Ballis

First Edition   ISBN 13: 978-0-692-73529-9

Contact the author at tess.ballis@gmail.com.

Edited by Jay Amberg. Cover photography by Katherine Evans. Designed & typeset by Sarah Koz. Set in Centaur, designed by Bruce Rogers in 1929, digitized by Monotype in 2000. Thanks to Nathan Matteson.

To Izzy and Will,
my first fans.

I

I HAVE ALWAYS THOUGHT of myself as strong. With my circumstances, I have no other choice. I've built myself a shell that cannot be cracked.

Sometimes, on nights like tonight, I shrivel into the nothingness underneath my shell. I curl up on my bed, pulling the thin blanket around me. If only there was a way to muffle the sound.

Dan and Renee, the people who gave birth to me, are going at it in the kitchen. Dan is too drunk to form proper words, but that's a common occurrence. Renee is pissed and is shrieking something, her shrill squawk and his low slur blending into madness.

They're my parents in only the most literal terms. Dan and Renee will never be my father and mother; they don't deserve it. Dan who drinks until he doesn't remember what he has done to himself, who brings his fists out and stains me black, blue, and red. Renee, emotionless, whose heart is encased in ice. Renee doesn't hit me, but her words are venom.

Their voices rise and fall, snapping and

screaming and stupidity. They hate each other almost as much they hate me.

Eden Wright, fifteen years old. Mommy and Daddy's little failure. The one thing I did wrong was to be born.

2

Here's their story: they met in college and began dating. It was more the choice of their parents; both of their parents had reputations to uphold. A little over a year later, Renee got pregnant. They wanted to get rid of *it,* that disgusting awful thing. Me.

Their parents firmly disagreed. They had to get married and keep the baby, so they could

TESS BALLIS

keep their reputations. It was either that, or they would be disinherited. That wasn't an option. Both of them were accustomed to spending on Mommy and Daddy's dime.

Dan and Renee hate me. They also can't stand each other. Every so often, Dan comes home marked with lipstick and unfamiliar perfume. Renee screeches and makes a huge deal out of it, but she always forgives him. Pathetic. Sometimes I wonder if it's because, somewhere deep down inside, she loves him.

No, Renee isn't capable of love.

3

I FALL ASLEEP TO THE wonderful sound of clashing words, shards of glass poking into each other. At least tonight there are no sharp words for me, because I've been an *ohsogood* girl by making myself disappear.

When I wake up Sunday morning, I creep out of bed silently. I wake up early on weekends

TESS BALLIS

to avoid Dan and Renee. Renee makes me feel about an inch tall, and Dan is…

I get ready as quickly as possible, a little game I like to play. But this game has consequences if I fail, a bleeding nose or a bleeding heart.

Usually it ends up being both.

Lacey, a senior at Maple Park High School where I'm a sophomore, is my only friend, but she's probably busy today. She has other friends, girls that smoke cigarettes and who knows what else, girls who wear thick black lines of eyeliner. She's probably hanging out with those girls today, and I don't like joining them.

I walk to the library, my go-to place. Meg, the librarian, is the only person besides Lacey who gives a shit about me.

"Hello, Eden," Meg calls out as I pass her. I give her a halfhearted wave and my shiny smile. She notices the lingering memories that flash in my eyes; I can tell by the pitying smile she always gives me. Still, she will never say anything about it. We've made a silent vow to seal this secret from the world.

I return my book, and Meg gives me another one she thinks I would like. This is our routine.

As soon as I open the book, someone taps my shoulder.

"Lacey!" I turn around and laugh.

Then I look at her face, and I gasp.

4

LACEY IS WEARING HER big sunglasses. For most people who pass by, big sunglasses don't send a red flag. I'm not most people; I know her better than that.

"Follow me," I hiss, and she lets me lead her to a remote corner without arguing.

"Take off your sunglasses," I demand, and she

obeys. She has a huge black eye, the bruise blossoming against her pale face.

"What did Rick *do?*" I ask firmly. Rick and Lacey have been dating since they were freshmen, a real love story. Well, Lacey loves Rick more than anyone has ever loved anyone. Rick claims he loves Lacey, but he doesn't always act like it. Rick has a short temper, and when he gets angry, Lacey has to wear her big sunglasses the next day.

"Don't you mean what did *I* do? I told him he had too much to drink." Bitter, hard words. Rick has hardened Lacey, who used to be sunshine and smiles. He's replaced her bubblegum with cigarette smoke and her chatter with unspeakable words. He has given her a horrifying story to tell.

Words freeze on the tip of my tongue. *You have to tell someone. Break up with him. Why do you let him do that?* These words will not do any good, and we both know it. Instead, I watch an unbreakable girl break.

"I can't do this anymore," Lacey whispers so quietly that I don't think she meant for me to hear.

"What do you mean?"

"He wants me to have sex with him," she states bluntly.

"He can't make you," I assure her gently, but that's not true. A memory flashes, brief and nauseating, and I gag.

I push the memory away; I like to ignore its existence. Even Lacey doesn't know what happened. No one will ever know.

5

Monday comes, rain tapping against the roof. School starts stretching on slowly, but at least it's not the house that will never be a home.

English class is right before lunch, and it's usually my favorite class. However, today's warm-up prompt makes my heart sink. PROMPT: WRITE ABOUT A FAVORITE FAMILY MEMORY.

Mrs. Hadley never checks our journals, so we can "write the truth." Bad Eden takes over and decides to really write the truth.

I was six years old, and my father staggered into the kitchen. He walked close to me, so close that I could smell the alcohol on his breath. Most six-year-olds can't detect this scent, but I knew it well. I closed my eyes and winced, knowing what was coming next. Instead of the pain I was expecting, his lips brushed my ear.

"You're a beautiful girl," he whispered, and I shrank back in fear. This wasn't the monster I knew, and I didn't like the way it felt when his lips were against my skin.

Something flashed in his eyes as I inched away. He slapped me, hard, and I cringed. This was the monster I knew.

I drop my pencil and stare at the words on

the page. Anger, sadness, betrayal, fear. The familiar feelings overwhelm me. They make me pick up my pencil and cross out everything I wrote.

As Mrs. Hadley tells us that our writing time is over, I notice that the page is dotted with tears.

6

Monday night, I hide under the thin blanket and enjoy the silence that surrounds me. It lasts for a long time, and then Renee lets out an earsplitting scream.

For a moment, my throat closes with panic. *Whathappenedwhathappenedwhathappened.*

"Dan, are you drunk on a Monday night?

Seriously?" Of course. That's what it is. Dan has arrived.

They shout for a while, and then Dan stomps up the stairs. Panic returns, paralyzing me. I wish Renee would come upstairs too, and I laugh at the thought that I would be more protected with her near. This is the woman who called me a worthless bitch before I could speak. She doesn't care when he slaps and punches and kicks, but I know that she minds the...other stuff.

Well, at least I think she does.

There's a sound of shattering glass, and I creep out of bed to get a look. I stand in the doorway of my bedroom and peek cautiously into the hall.

In front of Dan and Renee's bedroom, broken glass sits in a puddle of water. A single rose lies in the middle of the mess. Dan stands next to this disaster, fuming. He spots me and his eyes glint with anger, but anger is better than lust.

He walks over to me, and I run back to the safety of my bed. He steps into my bedroom. *No.*

He has not tried something in almost three years, but I can never trust him in my bedroom. Never.

He pulls my hair and whispers, "You better stay in here where you belong." Then he disappears.

I cling onto false security, but I can never be sure he won't do it again.

I was seven years old, and he walked into my bedroom.

"Daddy?" I whispered, pulling my blanket up to my chin. Something in his eyes was different tonight. He didn't look furious; he almost looked. . .hungry.

"You are such a pretty girl," he murmured.

I shivered at his voice, but the compliment made me feel good. Maybe he was going to love me after all. Maybe he was going to become the kind of daddy in books and TV shows.

"Thank you," I whispered.

"Do you love me?" he asked.

"Yes, Daddy."

"Show me. Show me you love me."

"How, Daddy?" I would do anything to make him love me, anything.

"Let me show you how."

I snap out of it when the nausea overwhelms me. I'm going to be sick.

That was the night he became Dan instead of Daddy.

7

LACEY ISN'T AT SCHOOL on Tuesday, and I'm concerned. I tell myself over and over that she is just sick. She probably has the flu or something.

Or something.

I can't seem to push other images out of my head. Sometimes her and Rick cut class together, and she usually comes back bruised.

Another disturbing thought nags me, because I know what Rick wants from Lacey. Is he...

He wouldn't. He does horrible things to Lacey, but not that. Even Rick wouldn't go that far to get what he wants from her.

Right?

8

On Wednesday, Lacey is back at school, bruise-free. Still, she seems a little off. She walks stiffly, her eyes are wide, and her face is ghostly white.

"Are you okay?" I ask for the third time.

"Eden, I'm fine!" she replies irritably.

"Just checking," I reply, squeezing her hand. It feels cold and clammy.

"What are you worrying about?" I whisper firmly.

"Rick and I have a date tonight, and I'm just kind of nervous about some...stuff."

"Don't go," I answer.

"I have to. I don't want him to be mad at me." When Lacey says things like that, she sounds so vulnerable. I see her as the girl with the blonde braids and missing teeth. Most people have forgotten that girl, maybe even Lacey herself, but I never will.

"You are going to be okay," I tell her

"How do you know?" Her voice quivers. She's frantic, begging.

"You are strong," I reply, and the words taste bitter, the aftertaste of a lie.

Rick killed my best friend. He turned her into *this.* The worst part is that he has made her think it's all her fault. Bad Lacey, too scared to speak up, all her fault.

Bad Eden, too scared to speak up. All my fault too.

9

WEDNESDAY AFTERNOON

I sit in the library, but I can't immerse myself into a fantasy world. The words are nonsense, floating around and cluttering my vision.

I close my eyes and imagine I am real girl with real parents. They wake me up on sixteenth birthday, and a car waits in the driveway. The

TESS BALLIS

beginning of a smile flits across my face, but it doesn't stay. Because I always remember.

"Honey?" Meg asks gently. "It's closing time." Disappointment flickers across my face, and she stares intently. Her warm brown eyes search for answers that I can't give her.

Renee is already in bed, and Dan isn't in the house when I arrive. I crawl into my bed without making a sound. This is the way I have to live, hiding in shadows and making myself disappear. Never allowed to exist.

Just as I'm drifting off, something hits the window. My heart races with fear as I peek outside. Lacey throws another rock at the window, and frantically waves her arms in the air.

I dash downstairs before she can shatter

the window, and I meet her outside. Lacey has curled into a ball, and she's shaking. The moonlight illuminates her face, showing scratches on her cheeks and a wild fear dancing in her eyes. The grass behind her is marked with vomit.

"Lacey——" I start, and she wraps her arms around me. She sobs into my shoulder, broken girl crumbling.

"You're okay," I whisper. "You're okay."

"No!" she screams out, jumping back as if I've slapped her.

"Lacey!" I call out.

"No, no, no!" she wails, tears streaming down her face. "I'm not!"

"I'm sorry, Lace. I just want you to be okay. That's all I want."

"Well, I'm not!" The look on her face is frighteningly familiar. I had a hunch before, but now I know what Rick has done. He has done exactly when Dan did to me years ago, exactly what destroyed me.

If I thought Lacey was destroyed before, I'm about to get a rude awakening.

10

"LACEY, I'M GOING TO help you, but I need you to tell me what happened." I try to keep my voice steady.

"He…he got what he wanted," she spits, cringing. I know what she means. I should call her parents or take her to a hospital or—

"Oh my god," I mutter. I'm going to throw up, flashbacks flickering in my head. Bloodstains on my nightgown, crying and begging, *pleasedaddyplease.*

"Eden?" Lacey asks quietly. I clutch my stomach and close my eyes. I'm going to implode if the memories don't go away.

Say it. Say it.

I love you, Daddy.

I want to stare right into her eyes and make her see the horrors etched into my skin. *Pleasedaddystop.* Instead, I just shake my head. It's not fair to her, not tonight.

Lacey hugging me, me hugging Lacey. Broken girls crying and giving up. Broken girls who are ghosts of the little girls they were, who will never be whole again.

11

On Thursday morning, Bad Eden decides she can't possibly go to school. Bad Eden picks up the phone and calls the school. *Hello, this is Renee Wright, Eden's mother. She has the flu, and she won't be coming to school today. Yes, I think it's going around. Thank you, good bye.*

Bad Eden sits in the library with Lacey, staring at the ceiling with empty eyes.

We sit in silence for hours and days and years, stretching on and suffocating me.

"I have a thought," Lacey finally speaks.

"What?"

"I want to..." her voice trails off, and she purses her lips.

"What? What, Lacey?" Irreversible damage has been done. The way her eyes droop, the way her shoulders are hunched, she's changed.

"I can't say it." Lacey shoots me an apologetic look, and then her whole body starts shaking. She curls up in a ball, rocking back and forth. Her eyes go out of focus. I grab her clammy hand and squeeze it, but she doesn't respond.

"Breathe," I beg frantically. Without Lacey, I have no one. No one. *You are a bad, selfish girl, Eden.*

You only ever think of yourself, and that is why everyone hates you. Renee is right about that after all; I'm only looking out for myself. I'm trying to drag Lacey back into life so I'm not alone.

I wonder, if she stops being broken before me, will I try to drag her back into darkness so I won't be alone there?

"I'm fine," Lacey mutters to her knees.

"What just happened?" I demand.

"I just panicked. I was going to tell you what I want to do, and then I got scared." Her innocence may be gone, but she's still as vulnerable as the little girl that withered away long ago. She seems so aged, and yet she has the wide eyes and dependency of a child.

"What do you want to do?" I cut in quickly.

"Die." It's whispered gently, and it takes a moment to register. It's just a word, but it's everything. It is a scared best friend taking a leap and leaving me stranded.

Lacey wants to die.

12

"EDEN?" LACEY WHISPERS hoarsely, waiting for the fog around me to clear up.

Suddenly I want to grab her shoulders and tell her every detail. She knows about the hitting and punching, the words that follow me like a trail of black smoke. She doesn't know that my innocence was stolen too.

I could tell her right now that I know begging and bleeding and being violated. *Dan did it to me too. I was seven the first time and thirteen the last time. He stopped because*——

"I have to go," I mumble.

"What?"

"I need to get out of here. Now." The tears feel wet and sticky as they trickle down my cheeks.

"We can do it together, dying," she offers weakly. Do I want to *die?*

"I—I can't." I'm too much of a coward to kill myself.

"Fine, but I found something that helps a little bit," she speaks up as I stand up.

"No alcohol. You know what it does to Dan."

"Painkillers," she replies.

"No," I start, but she still places a handful of pills into the palm of my hand. I close my hand around them and walk away wordlessly.

TESS BALLIS

13

I LEAVE THEM IN MY
sweatshirt pocket and try to forget them, but
they taunt me. Will I find relief, or will I end
up more troubled than Lacey?

I creep into the house, into my bedroom,
knowing Renee won't return home until tonight.
Regret threatens to suffocate me as I lay on
top of the bed. I should have told Lacey today.

I was thirteen the last time. I tried to hide under my blanket when I saw the look on his face. It meant it was going to be one of those nights when he wanted something else, something worse.

For the first time ever, Renee saw it happen. She stood in my doorway, expressionless, her face drained of color.

"Don't, Dan. Not that." With those few words, she walked away.

He never did it again, and I don't why she——

There's only one thing I can think of to not feel. Pill on my tongue. Gulp of water. Swallow. Let the world become fuzzy.

14

Lacey isn't at school on Friday. That's no surprise. I don't pay attention in any class, letting my mind wander instead. The pills made me numb and unaware, which is nice but unsafe for me. I need to be able to think and move fast when he comes home, so I need an alternate plan.

There's one more way to dull the pain, something I tried a few times when I was thirteen. I always thought it was crazy, but I probably am crazy anyway.

When I get home from school, I lock the bathroom door. Like I need to. Little girl pretending that there's someone on the other side of the door.

Razor kisses my wrists. My hips. Blood against skin.

Relief.

15

Blood stains the floor tiles, but I can't bring myself to care. What is the worst thing they can do to me? I let out a bitter laugh, and tears begin to flow.

I sink to the floor, crying and bleeding. I need to get out, out of this house and this life and *everything*.

I'm so sick of pretending, being a good girl

and letting them hurt me. It's time to lose control; I'm sick of fighting this downward spiral.

One pill, two pills down my throat.

Dry the tears, and leave a crimson stained bathroom. Not bleeding, still crying.

I'm done.

16

Days pass slowly, and I go through the motions. Lacey gives me pills that make me hurt less, but I will never not hurt.

School. Homework. Sleep. Hide. Listen to the aggressive shouts resonating throughout the house.

And the library. Pale yellow walls and cushy couches and Meg.

Meg with her gray hair in a perfect bun, with her kind eyes and warm smile. Maybe if I had a mother like her, I wouldn't be so screwed up.

But the library is temporary, small moments to savor, just enough to let me know what I'm missing. Not enough.

Two days before my sixteenth birthday, I wander into my quiet corner of the library to finish homework.

"Eden." I look up, startled. Meg places a book next to me.

"I haven't finished this one yet," I reply, holding a tattered paperback in the air.

"I know, but I think you will really like this one."

A shout forms on the tip of my tongue. *Wait!*

I need to tell you something. Take me far away, please. He hurts me. He hurts me, and I need to go away. Please, take me away.

I don't shout; I press it back inside where no one will see it.

"Thanks."

"I actually own this book. Bought it from the bookstore myself. I want you to have it. I want you to keep this."

"You don't have to do that."

"Please? For me?" Meg's voice is kind, but the words make me flinch. *He* said those words when I was nine, when lust and alcohol clouded his vision just enough.

Will he ever stop holding so much power over me?

A question forms on Meg's lips, but she just gives me a quick nod and heads back to her desk.

I skim the back of the book, catching words like girl, abused, strength. At first, all I feel is disappointment. I thought Meg would understand me enough to know a predictable book won't help.

Then, as I flip through the book, I notice something on the back page.

A phone number in Meg's messy scrawl. Underneath the phone number, she's written, "If you ever need help."

17

Dan bounds up the stairs, angrydrunk and ready to unleash the monster underneath his facade.

He opens the door to my bedroom, and my throat closes. He wouldn't try that kind of thing again.

I'm right. He grabs my shoulders, yells incomprehensible hatred, and shoves.

I fall.

My head slams against the hardwood floor, and everything blurs for a moment. As soon as he leaves, I sit up, dizzy. Tears stream out before I can stop them, because my head hurts, because this is my life, because it will never stop. There will never be a fairy tale happy ending. Hope only results in disappointment.

I grab the book from under my mattress, rip out the back page, and tear it into shreds.

18

WITH ONE DAY BEFORE my sixteenth birthday, I'm starting to think more and more like Lacey. Her words repeat in my mind. *What do you want to do, Lacey? I want to die.*

So I turn sixteen…and then what? Two more years of *this.* What comes after that? I have nothing: no future, no place to go.

Maybe her idea is my only option.

I don't tell her at school, though. This idea is something that's still taking shape.

Instead, I lock myself inside, keep my head down. No one notices anything different, but they never do. I am no one.

After school, I walk past the library without stopping. I can't even look at Meg, not when I know what Lacey and I might do. What it would do to her.

Walk into a silent house, ignore the ghosts in the corners. Crimson lines on my skin. Two pills, chalky on my tongue. Sleep.

Make it all go away. Soon it will go away forever.

TESS BALLIS

19

I WAKE UP TO THE SOUND of someone crying out at 3:00 AM.

"No, Daddy! Please!" someone screams, in the midst of a nightmare. I've screamed these words, in nightmares and in real life too. Begging for a father to be a father, yearning to escape the feeling of dissolving into nothing.

It's Renee.

She's a stranger to me, yet she's suddenly more familiar than ever. We're linked by our fear, our memories, by fathers who take what is ours.

Renee is broken too, and that is why she told Dan to stop. Renee is broken too, and all she did was tell Dan to stop.

She knows exactly how it feels, and she barely spoke up. Didn't care enough, and despite my fantasies, she never will.

Now I see her for who she is. She protects herself with ice because she's as scared as I am. I wish this was enough for me to forgive her, but Renee wasn't there for me when she saw father and daughter acting out her nightmares.

What have I done wrong? What is so desperately awful about me that makes her do this to me?

I just want to be enough.

20

Here's how to feel what I feel. Stare in a funhouse mirror, see a distorted image that is your own. Slide pieces of glass beneath your skin and let out soundless screams each time they cut you. See what's underneath, what's trying to claw its way out. See a heap of broken pieces, all the wrong pieces, and know. Know that there is nothing you will ever be able to do about it.

Go ahead and try to escape. Scream until your throat is raw. Climb on top of the highest mountain.

I guarantee, they will still never see you.

21

My sixteenth birthday starts with nothing. Dan and Renee are both sound asleep, side by side but not touching. I stand in their doorway, still and silent. My hand curls into a fist as I watch. Peaceful faces, eyes shut, never revealing who they really are.

I could kill them right now. I could grab a knife from the kitchen and kill them.

The thought crosses my mind, and I quickly push it away. That would be *crazy.*

Then again, am I not already crazy? If they were dead, they could never hurt me again.

I snap out of it after a moment. I'm *not* going to kill them. Killing = bad. I would leave just this prison for another. They deserve it, oh they deserve it so much, but I just can't do it.

I unclench my fist and leave without making a sound, becoming the shadow I need to be.

22

OF COURSE, THEY DON'T even know that I turn sixteen today; they never remember. Renee squeezes into crisp tailored clothes and hurries off to some brunch. It's Saturday, so Dan doesn't have work. He settles into the couch, holding a few beers.

I can't face the library, can't face Meg, but I

TESS BALLIS

can't stay either. *Daddythathurts. Pleasepleaseplease.*

Love me. Love me.

I will never let myself be home alone with him. Still, I don't know where I want to go. I pause in front of the door to consider my options.

"Eden," he mumbles from the couch as I am about to walk out the door. I hate my name when he says it. Every time it comes out of his mouth, it's enough to make me sick.

Ignore. Keep walking. The door is so close.

"Eden." He stands up, keeping one hand pressed against the wall for balance. Closer. Closer.

I want to run away from the imposing threat.

He may be bigger than me, but I'm more agile; I could easily run out the door. Panic sets in before I can escape, paralyzing me. Suddenly, I can't move, can't breathe, can't stop the nightmares playing in my mind.

I'm seven years old, and he has just done something bad. He has left me, and I stare at the stained sheets, too stunned to speak.

I'm nine years old, and I no longer wear pigtails because he loves innocence. It doesn't stop him.

I'm twelve, and I scream for help. Make so much noise that the neighbors are bound to hear. He holds me down and teaches me not to scream.

Today I'm sixteen, and it's been three years. He yanks me close to him, so close, and I gag. Why now, after all this time?

TESS BALLIS

"Don't," I whisper, tears brimming in the corners of my eyes. Around the age of eleven, my mind started taking me somewhere else when it would happen. In my mind, I would be at the beach. Today, I refuse to let myself drift away. I will fight him.

"Don't," I choke out again, and a scream climbs out of my throat. It hurts. Oh, it hurts, and this isn't just a bad dream and—

"Shut the fuck up," he growls. His hands, hot on my skin. His breath against my neck. He doesn't care that I wail out, nor does he care that my eyes glitter with hate and so much pain.

He takes what he wants from me. He takes and he takes, and he doesn't stop until he has had enough.

As I lay there shivering, he stands up. As nausea sweeps over me, he zips up his pants. As I throw up, he walks upstairs.

Words cannot describe the way it feels to be torn open.

23

WHEN I WAS YOUNGER I would clean up the stains, scrubbing until my fingertips were raw, a failed attempt to erase the previous events. Now I leave them there for the world to see. I hope Renee walks in and relives every damn memory. Something bitter and hard has formed in the hollow space in my chest.

I'm shaking all over, and the tears still have

not stopped. Done. Done done done with broken girl crying and waiting for it to get better. It never does.

Still trembling, I stumble into the bathroom. I need to take a shower. Now. The water is scalding, but it's not enough to take his fingerprints off my skin.

A hot shower and clean clothes aren't enough to make me not feel dirty, but they are a little bit calming,

Renee has a phone in her home office. She uses it for calling clients, and it sits on her desk.

I pick it up and dial Lacey's phone number. A pill or four will not make this go away, and I know that there's only one thing that will.

"Eden?" she murmurs sleepily into the phone.

"Yeah, it's me." It takes a moment to get the words out because my throat feels like it's closing.

"Happy birthday!" she squeals enthusiastically. In the forty minutes that have passed since a monster mumbled my name, I completely forgot about my birthday.

"I need—" I start, but the rest of the sentence won't come out.

"What?" she replies urgently.

"Do you remember what you said you wanted to do? That we could do it together? I'm ready if you still want to do it." My heart races. This is it. I'm sealing my fate.

There's a long pause before she replies, "Okay."

24

We meet at the library because I need to see Meg one last time. Guilt threatens to swallow me when Meg waves to me, but it's not enough to change my mind.

"Eden! I have a great book for you!" She smiles brightly.

"Actually I, um, just came to tell you something." I stumble over my words, trying to find the right combination. There are no words comforting enough to fix what we are going to do.

"What did you want to tell me?" she asks pleasantly, standing up from her desk chair.

"Thank you for…for everything," I start, on the verge of shattering.

"It's my pleasure," Meg replies, but her concern is thinly veiled.

"Well, you might not be seeing me for…" I stop, unsure of how to explain. "For a while. So, I wanted to say goodbye and thank you." Lacey squeezes my hand reassuringly.

"Girls, is there something going on? Do you need help?" she stares intently at us, exuding sympathy. The unasked question hangs in the air.

"No, we're fine," I jump in, just a little too quick. "I'm going to miss you. I just wanted to let you know."

Meg's floral perfume calms me as she pulls us in for a hug.

"Don't do anything you'll regret," she whispers in my ear, so quietly that I wonder if I'm just imagining it.

TESS BALLIS

25

Lacey walks outside without looking back, but I can't take my eyes off the door. I will never see this place again. As we turn the corner, Meg walks out of the library and heads to her car. That's strange; she rarely leaves one of the other librarians in charge, but I quickly forget. There are other things to worry about.

By the time we arrive at Lacey's house. my throat is closed with panic. Doubt whispers in my ear, at war with the memory of this morning replaying in my mind.

We stand in Lacey's bathroom, staring into her mother's medicine cabinet. I grab different pill bottles, driven by dread, but Lacey hangs back.

"I'm not so sure I want to do this," she confesses, glancing at me shyly. She leans on the edge of the bathtub, gripping it so hard her knuckles turn white. Angry eyes turn soft and syrupy, like something melts inside of her. Her lip quivers.

I picture Lacey on the playground when she was in third grade, her chin jutting out proudly,

and how quickly she could dissolve into someone so fearful. She never bothered hiding how
she felt, and tears weren't a symbol of surrender.

A sound bubbles out of my throat, almost
a laugh.

"What?" Lacey attempts to meet my eyes.

"You just kind of looked like...the old you,"
I explain, and it makes me ache. She is far from
the girl I once knew. Her syrupy eyes become
hard again, and she stares at me defiantly.

"I'm not anything like *her*. Actually, I changed
my mind. I want to do it."

26

I KNOW THAT WE HAVE TO move quickly before we lose our nerve. Armed with random bottles of pills and some vodka, we sit under a canopy of trees in Lacey's backyard.

"Let's get this over with," she states solemnly and begins unscrewing the lid to a bottle. We both reach for different bottles and pour them out in front of us.

"Eden, I love you like a sister," Lacey tells me, and then she reaches for the pile of pills in front of her.

"Me too," flies out of my lips.

She grabs handfuls, washing them down with vodka, and I have to stifle a scream. This is my best friend, and she's going to die. This is not how it should have ended. I don't want this for her, and yet I dragged her into it. It's too late now, so I follow her lead. I reach for the pills in front of me, round, white death sentences followed by vodka.

This is it. Death is at my fingertips, and I

just need to reach for it, but I can't. I think I'm scared. Time passes, suffocating and long, and everything is still.

"I'm afraid. Can you tell me a story?" Lacey whimpers. I open my mouth slowly, trying to find a memory that will make her last moments peaceful, and a story comes.

27

"Once," I begin. "There were two girls, Eden and Lacey. They met on the playground when Eden was in first grade and Lacey was in third grade. Lacey saw that Eden had a big bruise on her arm, but she didn't make of fun of Eden. No, instead she—"

28

It's vast and empty, just an endless expanse of black. The darkness seems to stretch on forever, and I keep walking. I'm not sure what I'm searching for, but I know I am searching.

It seems that I've been walking forever, but I don't want to stop. I'm not even scared. Actually, the darkness is calming, almost making me sleepy. The scent of Meg's floral perfume flits through the air.

Finally, I spot something blindingly white, and I'm filled with want as soon as I see it. Right away, I know that I need to follow the white light.

Every time I get close, it gets farther away. After repeated tries, frustration stops me. I decide to give up.

As soon as I've proclaimed this, the blackness dissolves.

29

"WHAT'S GOING ON?" I mumble sleepily as I open my eyes. For one blissful second, I can't remember anything, and then it all comes rushing back. Crap.

The hospital room is too bright, and the air is thick with the pungent scent of disinfectant. I cover my eyes with my hands.

"You're awake," a man, presumably the doctor, states.

"It didn't work," I respond without emotion. I'm relieved, disappointed, too many things to know how I feel. Just another failure, Bad Eden did something wrong again.

"Your stomach was pumped while you were unconscious. Do you know what pills you took?"

"I—I don't know." I stumble over my words.

"Well, you got lucky. You took quite a bit. You wouldn't be alive if you hadn't been found so quickly."

"How did I—"

The door swings open. A thin-lipped woman with ash blonde hair walks into the room.

"I'm Dr. Kline, the on-call psychiatrist," she explains, scrutinizing me from behind her eyeglasses. The other doctor slowly opens the door and slips out as she introduces herself.

"Who brought me here?" I assume Lacey's mother found us.

"I think her name was...Meg Hollis." Meg. I remember seeing her leave the library, the calming familiarity of her perfume. How far away that seems.

"Do my parents know?" I ask, even though the word "parents" tastes sour.

"They have been notified."

"What about Lacey?" It isn't until I ask that I realize how fearful I am of the answer. I didn't mean to bring Lacey into this mess, and she does not deserve to die. She's my best friend. How could I live without her?

"I'm sorry, but I don't know about your friend. I will be back shortly to ask you a few questions."

"Is she alive?" I beg frantically, but the doctor just walks out without even a sympathetic glance. A security guard stands outside my door, protecting me from myself. He does not understand that it's too late to protect me from the demons that have planted their roots inside of me. I lie there on the bed, shivering and lonely.

30

When Dr. Kline returns, she carries a laptop.

"I spoke to your mother. She signed the forms, so we have permission to treat you." As soon as she finishes, she jumps right into the interrogation.

She asks predictable questions and I give predictable answers. I manage to do so without giving anything away about what *he* does to me, and I barely even hint that he and Renee do not act like parents. I am just Average Sad Girl.

"We fear that you are a danger to yourself, so we are going to be keeping you in the psychiatric ward. You will be safe there, and you will get the help you need."

The words are generic and rehearsed; she doesn't understand a thing about me. She doesn't know what the real danger is. *Who* the real danger is.

I let Dr. Kline lead me down a long hallway without argument, a security guard trailing behind. I avert my eyes from the locked white doors we pass, and we finally come to a stop.

"Eden, I'm going to go now. I will see you

tomorrow in group therapy. Karen will be here if you need anything." She points to the nurse.

"Wait!" I call out as she turns around to leave.

"Yes?"

"Do you know what happened to my friend? Lacey Miller?" I ask again, hoping that she will tell me what I need to hear. I know that this is foolish, hope never works out for me, but it's all I have.

"I'm sorry, that information is confidential," she responds before walking away.

31

As I enter the ward, I examine everywhere, desperate to see Lacey. I don't.

The room is almost bare. Steely-eyed nurses and guards watch my every move, and no one will tell me what happened to Lacey.

Cold and alone, I try to drift off to sleep, but it doesn't come. I use the stiff pillow to muffle my cries. As if someone would come if they heard. Far away from the house that is not a home, I'm still playing pretend.

32

GROUP THERAPY IS A JOKE, which is what I expected. As soon as I sit down, I realize that I'm going to have to put on an act. There is absolutely no way I am telling these people anything.

I count eight other people sitting in little plastic chairs, nine including Dr. Kline.

Lacey isn't one of them.

When Dr. Kline asks me to speak, I do, but almost none of it is the truth. Instead, I feed them lies about a sad little girl who is so much more sane than me.

If only they knew.

33

EACH MINUTE, HOUR, DAY passes. The plan is that I will be discharged after three days and go home to my parents. I still haven't told anyone about them.

On the third day, Dr. Kline pulls me aside after group therapy.

"You get to make a phone call today," she tells me.

"I know."

"Are you excited?"

I just shrug in response. I'm not sure.

I'm not nervous at all, not until the phone is in my hand. Once I'm about to make the call, my fingers start to tremble.

I call the library, and Meg answers right away.

"It's Eden. I'm calling from the hospital."

There's a slight pause before she finally speaks. "Ah, I've been waiting to hear from you. I'm so glad you called."

34

"Do you know what happened to Lacey?" I press before she can get another word in.

"Honey, I'm not sure I—"

"Please. I just need to know this one thing. Is she alive?"

"I'm so sorry." Her voice is tinged with dread, and I know right away.

No. This isn't happening, just one of my nightmares. A sound comes out of my mouth, halfway between a scream and a sob.

"I know, trust me, but I need you to listen for just a moment. If someone is hurting you at home, you cannot go back there. You and me, we'll figure it out."

I'm prepared to lie. I plan to reassure her that everything is fine, thanks for the concern, but that is not what happens.

"Please don't let him hurt me again," I whisper. It's a plea, a confession. It's me letting go of the secret that has been hidden deep inside for nine years.

35

LACEY IS THE ONLY THING on my mind for the rest of the day. I sit on my bed, reliving every memory we shared. Nobody knew the girl I knew, not even her mother. I knew a girl who was daring, compassionate, and kind. A girl who became someone childish, insecure, and most of all, scared.

Lacey would want me to tell. Tomorrow, my

release day, Meg is coming. I will tell her every-thing. I won't tell Dr. Kline because I don't know how the rules with child services work, but I'll make sure Meg knows. I'm going to make sure I'm safe. I would even testify in court if it meant *he* would be put behind bars. We're going to make it happen.

The thought of speaking up frightens me, but there's something else too, something very rare for me.

As I drift off to sleep, I feel hope, real, pure, hope.

TESS BALLIS

36

DR. KLINE TAKES ME TO the waiting room, expecting to see Renee there to pick me up, but she isn't there yet. Big surprise. Meg is there, sitting in a waiting room chair.

"Can I talk to my friend?" I ask, and Dr. Kline nods halfheartedly, sneaking a glimpse at her watch.

As soon as I approach Meg, she stands up and hugs me, and I breathe in the scent of flowers.

"I am so sorry about Lacey." Her voice is soft, nearly a whisper.

"I have to tell you something," I blurt out. I need to say it now before I get too nervous.

"Tell me."

I do. Words flow, stories that have been hidden underneath, secrets I have never shared. They just spill out until the weight on my chest is lifted. I keep my quivering voice low, so we are not overheard.

"Don't cry, Eden. You're safe now." Meg leans forward to wipe away the tear cascading down my cheek.

TESS BALLIS

"I don't know what to do," I whimper, scared little girl shrinking back because her daddy has so much power.

"I would love for you to stay with me, if you want to. All my kids are away at college, and the house just feels so empty. No one will ever hurt you there." A wistful smile settles on her lips.

"If you would have me, I would love to." I dig my nails into my skin to make sure I'm awake. Life will never have a happy ending; there must be some catch. I'll wake up from this dream soon.

"I promise, we are going to fix this," Meg assures me, and then Renee walks in.

37

SHE GRIMACES AS SHE walks in like she is disgusted. She pulls off her designer sunglasses, revealing tired bloodshot eyes.

"Let's go!" she exclaims in an overly sweet voice.

"Wait, there are some things we need to discuss first." Dr. Kline grabs Renee's frail wrist before she can turn around. Renee smiles stiffly and lets Dr. Kline talk about safety plans, outpatient programs, medication.

When Dr. Kline is done, Renee eagerly hurries out before her facade can slip away. She hides her ugliness well, but it doesn't fool me.

As soon as we're outside, a switch flips in my mind. The things Renee and *him* do to me are not my fault; they control their actions. It is what's wrong with them, not what's wrong with me. I need to break the silence. I take a deep breath, gather all of my courage, and look right at her.

"I'm telling."

38

"Excuse me?" she hisses, color draining from her face.

"I'm telling the police what he did to me. I'm going to live with Meg the librarian because she actually gives a damn about me." I'm not scared. Actually, I feel lighter than ever.

"You don't know anything. Shut your—"

"No. Do you remember what you walked in when I was thirteen. That other *thing* he did to me? Well, guess what? He started that when I was seven. He stopped after you told him to stop. Well, until a few days ago."

"I told you to shut—"

"I'm not finished!" I screech. "I know your father did it to you too."

"How could you possibly know that?" she snarls, flinching.

"I heard you crying out in your sleep. Are you going to deny it?"

"If you knew what was good for you, you would shut up right now."

"No, I'm done with that! You know what

it's like, you *know*, and still you let him do it to me. How could you? What is it that makes me so repulsive in your eyes?"

"Stop!" she wails, but the panicked look on her face makes me feel no pity. She brought this on herself, and I am angry. So, very angry.

"I am telling the police, and you can't stop me."

"He will go to prison for a while," she responds quietly.

"Yes."

"I could face charges too."

"Yes."

As I turn to walk back into the hospital, back to Meg, she murmurs something that almost sounds like sorry.

TESS BALLIS

39

IT'S BEEN SIX MONTHS and thirteen days since I tried to kill myself, and it's the first time I've gathered enough courage to visit Lacey's grave.

I didn't go to the funeral; I couldn't handle it. I knew that I wouldn't even be able to look at her mother. Her daughter is gone, and I'm still here, and she should hate me for living. Maybe I wasn't ready then, but I am now.

"Are you sure?" Meg asks one more time.

"I'm sure." I open the door and slide out of her car, my hands trembling. Panic threatens to envelop me as I spot the tombstone with her name.

I set down the bouquet of violets I've been holding, amidst the many roses. Everyone brought roses.

Violets were her favorite.

A few people have propped up flimsy photographs, pictures of her with her heavy make-up and fiery eyes. Her smile doesn't look real in any of them, and a sob swells in my throat. It's not fair. She pictured death as something beautiful and poetic, but that isn't how it goes. She didn't realize how permanent it was, how final. This isn't what she wanted.

But it's too late now.

I need to stay; I need closure, but I can't.

No, I can. There are so many things I can't do. Sleep through the night. Control the way my heart races when something triggers a rush of memories. Say his name, or even think it, even though he's in prison now and can't hurt me.

This is something I can do.

"Goodbye, Lacey," I whisper solemnly. Before I leave, I place a small picture down beside the other photographs, not something anyone would notice.

In the picture, two little girls are holding

hands. One has straight brown hair and a faded bruise on her cheek. The other has two blonde braids and an earsplitting grin.

Two little girls with no broken pieces.

BROKEN GIRLS

ACKNOWLEDGEMENTS

First & foremost, thank you to Dr. Jay Amberg for giving me the opportunity and for helping me grow as a writer. I'm so grateful for the experience. Thank you to Sarah Koz for turning a manuscript written on a Word document into a real book, for turning it into a reality. To Steve, for helping me to not feel broken myself and for encouraging me to put those feelings into writing. Thank you to all of my proofreaders for drastically improving my writing. Lastly, thank you to my family, not only for showering me with support, but for being the farthest from Eden's family that a family can get.

ABOUT THE AUTHOR

TESS BALLIS is fourteen years old. She likes writing poetry and stories. When she isn't writing, she likes to listen to music, read, sing, and play the piano. *Broken Girls* is her first novel.

www.ingramcontent.com/pod-product-compliance
Lightning Source LLC
Chambersburg PA
CBHW071325130626
46556CB00004B/1754